Max and the Baby-sitter

Danielle Steel
Max and the Baby-sitter

Illustrated by Jacqueline Rogers

Delacorte Press

Published by
Delacorte Press
Bantam Doubleday Dell Publishing Group, Inc.
666 Fifth Avenue
New York, New York 10103

Library of Congress Cataloging in Publication Data
Steel, Danielle.
Max and the baby-sitter / by Danielle Steel ; illustrated by
Jacqueline Rogers.
p. cm.
Summary: Unhappy with the baby-sitter he has, four-year-old Max
is relieved when his parents find him a baby-sitter he likes much
better.
ISBN 0-385-29796-3
[1. Baby-sitters—Fiction. 2. Parent and child—Fiction. 3. New
York (N.Y.)—Fiction.]   I. Rogers, Jacqueline, ill. II. Title.
PZ7.S8143Max   1989
[E]—dc19   88-35252
                                                CIP
                                                AC

designed by Judith Neuman-Cantor

Manufactured in the United States of America

November 1989

10 9 8 7 6 5 4 3 2 1

To Vanessa, sweet little tiny baby girl
Daddy and I love so much!

Love,
Mommy

This is Max. He is four years old and he lives in New York. His Daddy is a fireman and his Mommy is a nurse.

Sometimes he goes to the firehouse with his Daddy. It's a lot of fun to see the fire trucks, the ladders, and the pole his Daddy and the other firemen slide down when the alarm sounds and they have to go to a fire.

Max also goes to visit his Mommy at the
hospital. She works in the part of the hospital
where new babies are born. It's fun to look
in the nursery window and see them.
The babies in the nursery are very little.

On some days when Max's Mommy is at work, his Daddy picks him up at school and takes care of him at home. They go to the grocery store, or the park to play ball or walk to the river and look at the boats. Once they even went to the Empire State Building.

And on days when Max's Mommy and Daddy both work, he goes to his baby-sitter. Her name is Jean, and she's really nice, and he likes going there a lot.

When Max was three years old, his Mommy and Daddy used to take him to a different baby-sitter, named Barbara. Sometimes she was nice, but sometimes she shouted at the children she took care of. Sometimes it was too cold in her house. She had a cat who scared him, too.

When Max went home at night, he would cry a lot. He had nightmares. He had bad dreams about Barbara's cat. He was afraid it would scratch him. His Daddy would hold him and make him feel better.

When Max's Daddy is at the firehouse,
Max's Mommy takes him to school. They bake
cookies, or ride the Staten Island ferry.

Max's Mommy and Daddy were sad that he didn't like going to Barbara's house. It made them feel terrible to see him crying when they left him there. They knew that Barbara was a nice lady. They couldn't understand why Max was so unhappy about going to the baby-sitter's.

Finally, one day, trying to stay calm, and without even crying once, Max explained it to them. He told them how her house was always too cold, and how scared he was of her cat, and how she shouted at the children sometimes, and how the lunches she made were always yucky.

Max's Mommy and Daddy talked about it for a long time. They didn't want Max to be unhappy. Maybe Barbara's house just wasn't the right place for Max. So they started visiting other baby-sitters.

And while they were looking, a little part of Max hoped that they wouldn't find any baby-sitter at all. His Mommy would stay home to take care of him and stop working. Then they could bake cookies every day, and visit the Statue of Liberty, and ride on the Staten Island ferry. But Max's Mommy explained that she couldn't stay home all the time, even though she would have liked to.

After a few weeks, Max's Mommy and
Daddy said they wanted him to meet Jean.
She lived only four blocks away from
Max's house. Max could smell something
delicious in the hall when they rang the
doorbell. And sure enough, when she opened
the door, Jean had just taken a tray of
chocolate chip cookies out of the oven.
She offered one to Max and it was yummy.
Then she took him inside and introduced
him to the other children. There were two
little girls and another little boy, and outside
her kitchen there was a pretty little garden.

There were lots of toys to play with, and every afternoon, after their nap, Jean read the children a story. She had paints and modeling clay, too, and they made puppets out of papier-mâché, and on special holidays, they made presents for their Mommies and Daddies.

And if anyone had a birthday,
Jean made a birthday cake, and they all
decorated it, and before they ate it,
everyone sang "Happy Birthday."

"Do you have a cat?" Max asked. He liked it here right away, it was warm and friendly and cozy. And Jean looked like a nice lady.

"No." Jean smiled. "I don't have a cat, but I have a little friend you might like to meet out in the garden." She took Max's hand and walked out to the garden. There, asleep in a little basket under a tree, was a brown and white puppy. Jean picked him up gently and let Max hold him. When they went back to the kitchen, Max saw that Jean had goldfish, a parakeet, a hamster, and a bunny.

"I like it here." Max smiled up at his Mommy and Daddy. "I like Jean," he whispered when she went to help the other children.

"So do I," Max's Daddy said. And Max's Mommy was smiling too. They both wanted Max to be happy.

Max's Mommy and Daddy wanted to leave him with a baby-sitter he liked, and where they knew he'd be happy and safe and comfortable while they were working. They were glad to know why he hadn't been happy with Barbara. They were happy they'd found Jean and that Max liked her.

The next day, when Max's Mommy and
Daddy had to go to work, his Mommy walked
him to Jean's house. He skipped all the
way. There were delicious smells when
they got to her front door. She was baking
blueberry pie for them to eat with vanilla
ice cream after naptime. The little girls

were making paper dolls and the little
boy was helping to take care of the
hamster. As soon as Max took off his
jacket, Jean asked him if he would help
feed the puppy.

Max had a busy day at Jean's house. He had so much to do that he was surprised when he saw his Daddy waiting for him in the doorway.

"Time to go home?" Max looked surprised. "So soon?"

"Yes." Daddy smiled. "You've been here since early this morning. I thought we'd pick Mommy up at the hospital and go out for dinner."

It sounded like a great idea to Max, so Jean helped him put on his jacket. She gave him all the pictures he had drawn for

his Mommy and Daddy. Max kissed her
good-bye, and waved as they went out the
door. When he went out to dinner, he told
them all the things he and Jean and the
other children had done since that morning. He
could hardly wait to go back to Jean's house.

That night when he went home, Max's
Mommy gave him a bath.

His Daddy tucked him into bed and kissed him good night. Max fell asleep almost before his Daddy left the room, with a happy smile, dreaming of Jean, and her puppy.

Quality Printing and Binding by:
Ringier America, Inc.
16515 West Rogers Drive
New Berlin, WI 53151-2298 U.S.A.